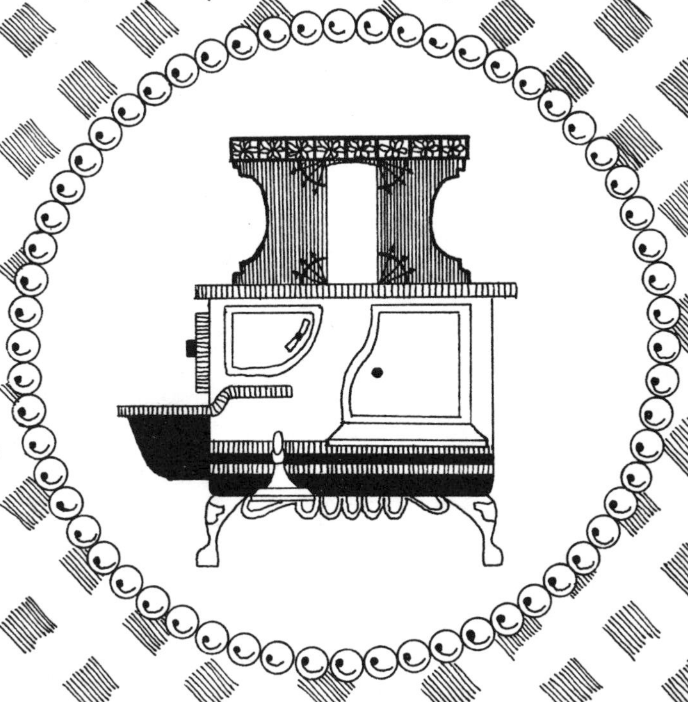

WHERE'S FLORRIE?

WHERE'S FLORRIE?

By Barbara Cohen
Illustrated by Joan Halpern

Lothrop, Lee & Shepard Company
A Division of William Morrow & Company, Inc.

New York

Books by BARBARA COHEN

The Carp in the Bathtub

Thank You, Jackie Robinson

Where's Florrie?

1   2   3   4   5   80   79   78   77   76

Library of Congress Cataloging in Publication Data

Cohen, Barbara.
    Where's Florrie?
    SUMMARY: Florrie makes her stern father angry by building a fire in her toy stove, but by the end of the day she finds out Papa really loves her after all.
    [1. Fathers and daughters—Fiction] I. Halpern, Joan. II. Title.
PZ7.C6595Wh   [Fic]   75-40341
ISBN 0-688-41738-8   ISBN 0-688-51738-2 lib. bdg.

For my mother, Florence Nash

One year Mama and Papa gave me a stove for my birthday.

It was just like Mama's, only much, much smaller. It was made out of black cast iron. It had a chimney and little grooved lids that lifted off with a separate handle. It came with its own set of black cast iron pots and pans. In front, it had doors that opened. Inside, you were supposed to build a fire out of coal, and light it with a match. Then you could really cook.

"Oh, thank you! Thank you!" I shouted when I opened the package at breakfast on the morning of my birthday. I had wanted that stove more than anything. I had been looking at it in the window of Kaufmann's Variety Store for six months, ever since Mr. Kaufmann had put it there. I was so happy to get it that I ran up to Mama and threw my arms around her and hugged her tight.

Papa was there, too. It was too early for him to open his tavern. I hardly ever saw Papa. He worked in the tavern until very late at night, and he was usually still asleep when I left for school or went out to play. But the morning of my birthday he had breakfast with us.

After I was done hugging Mama, I turned to Papa. "Thank you, Papa," I said. "Thank you for the stove." I spoke softly. I was afraid of Papa.

Papa looked at me with his hard blue eyes. "Listen to me, Florrie," he said. "Listen to me very, very carefully. You must never, ever build a fire in that stove. If you do we will take it away from you. We'll take it back to

13

Kaufmann's Variety Store and I will be *very, very* angry!"

"I can't build a fire, Papa," I said. "Mama keeps the matches on the top shelf of the kitchen closet. I can't even reach them if I stand on a chair."

Papa stood up. He was so tall he almost reached the ceiling. His shoulders were so broad they filled the doorway.

"I don't care," he said to me sternly, "whether you can build a fire or you can't build a fire. Just DON'T build a fire." And then he stalked out of the kitchen.

"He's mean," I said to Mama angrily. "He's always mean to me."

Mama kissed me. "No, he isn't, Florrie. It's just that he has so much on his mind. Papa loves you."

But I didn't believe her. I didn't believe he loved me at all. He had spoiled my birthday. What was the use of a stove just like Mama's if I couldn't cook on it?

We lived in the back of Papa's tavern on the corner of Barbey Street and Sutter Avenue in

East New York. In those days, long, long ago, I used to sit on the stoop in front of the tavern playing with my dolls and my stove. I always found odds and ends of trash on the street that I could put in the pots and pretend to cook up for the dolls' dinner. Sometimes Gladys would come down from the flat above the tavern and play with me. Gladys was two years older than I, and she certainly wasn't crazy about me, but no one had ever given *her* a cast iron stove.

Gladys wanted me to light a fire in that stove in the worst way. But she couldn't want it any worse than I did. I wanted to cook — to really cook, like Mama.

One hot summer evening before supper when Gladys and I had been playing on the stoop for a while, she said, the way she always did, "Come on, Florrie, let's build a fire in the stove."

"I can't build a fire, Gladys," I said the way I always did. "You know Papa won't let me build a fire."

"I dare you to build a fire," Gladys said.

There wasn't very much I wouldn't do on a dare. But still I said no.

"Scaredy cat, scaredy cat," Gladys began to chant. "Florrie's just a baby scaredy cat."

"If you had a Papa like mine," I said, "you'd be scared too. Papa can give a terrible whipping." Papa had never whipped me in his life. Sometimes when I got in her way, Mama slapped at my legs with a dish towel, but Papa had never laid a hand on me. I guess to me his look when he was angry seemed worse than a whipping.

"Your Papa doesn't even have to know," Gladys whispered. She had never said that before. Usually the line about Papa's whippings shut her up. "He's so busy today he'll never come out on the stoop."

That was true. It was so hot that it seemed as if every family on the block was sending someone over with tin pails in which to carry home ice cold beer, or root beer, which Papa

sold too. He was so busy filling those pails and serving the men who drank their beer right in the tavern that I was sure he'd never get a chance to come out on the stoop to smoke his cigar. As for Mama, she was in the back with the baby. She was always in the back with the baby.

"And what if he does come out?" Gladys continued. "I'll tell him it was my idea. I'll tell him I made you do it!"

I wanted to. I wanted to, more than anything. But how could I? "I don't have any coal," I said.

"Coal?" said Gladys. "Coal? Who needs coal? I'll go behind Zuckerman's Grocery and get slats from one of those wooden crates he throws back there. And we'll break it up into little pieces and that's what we'll burn in the stove."

"Well," I said, "go ahead. Go ahead and get the wood."

So she went. While she was gone, I broke up a chocolate bar Mama had given me earlier and I put bits of it into each of the pots. I figured we could cook that. It would melt down into nice cocoa for the dolls, even if it was too hot for cocoa.

After a little while, Gladys came back with the strips of wood from the vegetable crates. It took us awhile to hack them up and we both got a few splinters in our hands.

When we were done, I looked at Gladys and Gladys looked at me. "Well, Gladys," I said, "I haven't got a match." I felt relieved that we couldn't actually light a fire, but I felt sorry too.

"Oh, don't worry about that," Gladys said. "I'll go up and get some from our flat. No one's home."

I hardly had time to open the little door and lay some of the pieces of wood inside the stove when Gladys was back down with a box of matches. She tossed them in my lap.

"Go ahead," she said. "Light it."

"Me?" I said. "Me? I don't know how to light a match. I never lit a match in my life. You do it."

"Naw," said Gladys. "It's your stove. You ought to light it." She looked down and scraped the toe of her shoe against the edge of the stoop. I suddenly got the idea that Gladys had never lit a match in her life either.

Just then Morrie Weissbinder came out of the tavern. He had gone in when Gladys was upstairs getting the matches. Gladys liked Morrie Weissbinder. "Hi, Morrie," she said.

"Hi, Gladys," he replied. "Hey, you want to help me? You want to help me carry this pail of

root beer home? If you do, I'll bet Ma'll let you have a glass of it."

"Sure, Morrie," Gladys said. "Sure, I'll help you." Morrie set the pail down, and the two of them picked it up, each holding one side of the handle, and set off down Sutter Avenue, trying not to let the pail swing too much as they walked.

So there I was, all alone, with a stove full of wood and a box of matches on my lap. I opened the box. I looked at the big wooden match sticks lying side by side in the box, so neat and regular. I looked at them for quite a long time. Then I took one out. I closed the box. I struck the match, hard and sharp against the edge of my stove, as I had seen Mama do a thousand times. Sure enough it burst into a bright flame, orange around the edges and blue in the middle.

I thrust the match inside the stove door. I dropped it on the little pile of wood and pulled my hand out.

The wood caught. But it didn't make a pleasant, rosy fire like the coal in Mama's stove. It burst into flames, and in a moment the flames were pouring out of the chimney and out of the door and out from around the edges of the grooved lids the pots were sitting on.

I jumped up and stood back against the building. I put my fingers in my mouth. I felt as if my eyes would pop out of my head. I couldn't make a sound.

Just then the door of the tavern swung open. Out on the stoop came—Papa! There was the stove, blazing away, and me, splattered against the wall as if someone had thrown me there. Papa took it all in with one glance.

"Florrie!" he said sharply. Then he reached out to grab me. He was quick, but I was quicker. I jumped off the stoop and ran down Sutter Avenue as fast as my feet could carry me. But though I was quick, I wasn't quick enough. My legs were too short. I knew my father would catch up with me very soon.

I had a head start, though. He had to turn around, push open the swinging doors, and shout to someone inside to come with water and put out the fire. Then he took off after me.

Everybody was out on the street that evening. It was too hot to stay in the apartments. I dodged in and out among the long cloth legs of the men, the long rustly skirts of the women.

Then, in a burst of inspiration, I turned into a narrow alley between two tall tenements, and crouched down behind one of the garbage pails that nearly blocked the entrance into the alley.

I peered out around the garbage pail and, sure enough, very soon I saw a pair of white flannel legs tear by. It was my father. He always was a very smart dresser. After he passed, I counted to a hundred. I made myself count very, very slowly. Then I came out of the alley. I could no longer see Papa in the crowds that moved up and down the street, but I was sure he had gone straight on down Sutter Avenue. I was sure that he had not turned the corner which was only a few yards beyond the alley in which I had hidden. So I turned the corner.

I had never been on that street before. It was narrower than Sutter Avenue, but just as busy. I ran down it for a couple of blocks, still dodging the crowds. Then I slowed down. I was tired of running, and I knew I'd escaped from Papa. But I kept on walking. I didn't stop.

After awhile, I began to hear some music. I recognized the tune. I began to sing the words

softly to myself as I walked toward the music.

Meet me in St. Louis, Louis,
Meet me at the fair.
Don't tell me the lights are shining
Any place but there.
We will dance the Hoochee Koochee,

I will be your tootsie wootsie,
If you will meet me in St. Louis, Louis,
Meet me at the fair.

At the next corner, I found the music. It was from a carousel, a merry-go-round, mounted on a wagon pulled by a big old horse.

The carousel was the most beautiful thing I had ever seen. The horses were pink and red and yellow and orange. Their manes were gold and silver, their necks were arched, their eyes were bright, their hooves pawed at the ground. There were four of them on that carousel, and round and round they went, while the music played.

Meet me in St. Louis, Louis,
Meet me at the fair . . .

When the carousel man stopped turning the crank, the horses were still. The four children who had been riding on their backs climbed down. The real horse tossed the feathery red plumes on his head and moved on. I followed.

"Carousel! Carousel!" the man cried. "Come ride the carousel! Come ride the carousel!"

After awhile, he stopped the wagon again. Four more children gave him nickels and he helped them climb up on the backs of the make-believe horses. Again he began to crank, and again round and round went the horses.

Don't tell me the lights are shining
Any place but there . . .

I forgot about the stove. I forgot about the fire. I forgot about Papa. My mind was filled with the carousel. I didn't even envy the children who were riding on it. I didn't even wish I had a nickel. It was enough to be near it, to follow it, as if in a dream, through the streets.

Night was coming on. Even in summer, daylight doesn't last forever. I don't know how many times the man stopped the carousel, helped off one set of children, and helped on another set of children, clutching their nickels. But I followed him. I followed him all the while. All the other children kept changing, changing. Only I remained.

Then it got too dark. There were no more children on the street. Their mothers had called them in. It was time for the man and his carousel to go home.

The carousel man looked down at me. He must have noticed me before, but now he spoke to me.

"Do you want a ride, little girl?" he asked. "Do you want a ride before we go home?"

"I don't have a nickel," I said.

"That's O.K.," he said. "Have a ride anyway.
Which one do you like?"

"The orange one," I said. I could hardly
breathe, I was so excited. "I like the orange
one."

He was not a big man, but he swung me up
on the orange horse easy as singing. Then he
began to crank, and the carousel began to go

around. Around and around with only me on it. All that music pouring out into the warm night air, just for me.

> We will dance the Hoochee Koochee,
> I will be your tootsie wootsie,
> If you will meet me in St. Louis, Louis,
> Meet me at the fair.

I don't know how long the ride lasted. Maybe five minutes, maybe half an hour. It was a dream. In a dream, there is no time.

It was quite, quite dark when the carousel stopped. The man lifted me down. "That's it, little girl," he said. "Time for me and Sally here to get along home."

"Thank you," I said. "Thank you very much."

"Oh, that's all right. Maybe next time I'm out this way you'll be able to put your hands on a nickel."

"Oh, I hope so."

"Well, then, good night."

"Good night."

I sat down on the curb. There was no music any more, but I listened for as long as I could hear the wagon wheels rolling along and Sally's hooves clip-clopping in the darkness. After awhile the sounds died away.

The street was empty and silent. I looked around me. I wasn't on a busy avenue lined with stores and apartment buildings like the one I lived on. All I saw were one-family houses, each with its own lawn, its own fence, and its own tree. Except for a dog barking somewhere, it was very quiet. Then even the dog stopped barking.

Suddenly I realized I was lost. I ran down to the corner and looked at the street sign under the lamp post. Sackman Street. But I had never heard of Sackman Street. I didn't know how to get home from Sackman Street. I didn't know where I was.

The light from the street lamp was a pool, surrounded by thick blackness. I had never been out alone in the empty night.

I didn't know what to do. My legs were so tired I couldn't stand on them any longer. I just sat on the curb and put my head down on my arms. I didn't believe in crying, but tears began to creep down my cheeks. Even though the night was warm, I shivered in the dimness.

I don't know how long I sat there. I think I had almost sobbed myself to sleep when I felt someone touch my shoulder. I let out a little startled scream and looked up.

It was Papa.

I could see him in the lamplight. It was Papa.

"Florrie," he said, very softly. "Will you come home now, Florrie?"

"Yes, Papa," I said. I wasn't frightened. I was glad to see him. "I'm tired."

He picked me up in his arms. I nestled my head against his cheek. I could feel wetness on it.

"You're a tough bird, aren't you, Florrie?" he said. "Just like your old man."

He carried me all the way home. He carried me right into our kitchen and set me down on a chair. A lot of people were there when we first came in, but I was too tired to notice them much. Soon they had all left.

Mama told me I had been a naughty girl, but all the time she hugged me and kissed me. She washed my face with a damp cloth and then she gave me pot roast and apple sauce and hot tea with lots of milk and sugar in it. I was so hungry that I ate it all up and then I went to sleep.

Papa never scolded me for building the fire. He never scolded me for running away. He didn't even take the stove back to Kaufmann's Variety Store. But he did put it on the top shelf of the kitchen closet for a whole year before he let me play with it again.

I didn't like that very much. There were still a lot of things about my Papa that I didn't like very much. But never again did I think he didn't love me. Not even for one second.